MW00905311

CHUKUMS, CHARLIE AND CALI

Fur-Ever Family

By: Julia E. Giancaspro

Illustrated by: stefanie st. denis

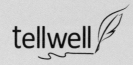

tellwell

Chukums, Charlie and Cali
Copyright © 2024 by Julia E. Giancaspro

All rights reserved. No part of this publication may be reproduced, distributed, or transmitted in any form or by any means, including photocopying, recording, or other electronic or mechanical methods, without the prior written permission of the author, except in the case of brief quotations embodied in critical reviews and certain other non-commercial uses permitted by copyright law.

A special thank you for the writing assistance provided by Karen Stephenson of The Happy Guy Marketing Inc.

Tellwell Talent
www.tellwell.ca

ISBN
978-1-77941-477-9 (Paperback)

Chukums and Charlie are sister Chihuahuas who love their happy home with Mommy and Daddy. They are best friends "fur-ever," and nothing will ever get in the way of that!

One day, Chukums and Charlie are cuddled together waiting for Mom and Dad to come home. When they hear the car pull into the driveway, Charlie jumps up. Chukums wags her tail. They bark with excitement as they look out the window, "Woof! Woof! Woof!"

"Oh no!" says Chukums. Their barking stops as they see Mom and Dad getting a cat out of the car. What is even worse, is that they are walking to the front door with this cat!

The door opens. Chukums and Charlie start to growl, "GGGrrrrrr..." They do not like cats!

"Chukums and Charlie, this is your new sister, Cali! She is now part of our family," Dad explains.

Cali is an American bobtail cat. She has a short tail. She has tufted ears and toes and a powerful body.

Chukums and Charlie stop growling. They drop their heads low, as Mom sits on the living room floor with Cali.

"Chukums and Charlie, come say hello to your baby sister," Mom calls.

Very slowly, feeling uneasy, they do. Cali softly meows to greet Chukums and Charlie. They each sniff Cali from head to toe and walk away. Feeling displeased, Chukums turns toward Charlie. "Huff! Not only is going for our walkies not happening, but this cat is also here to stay!"

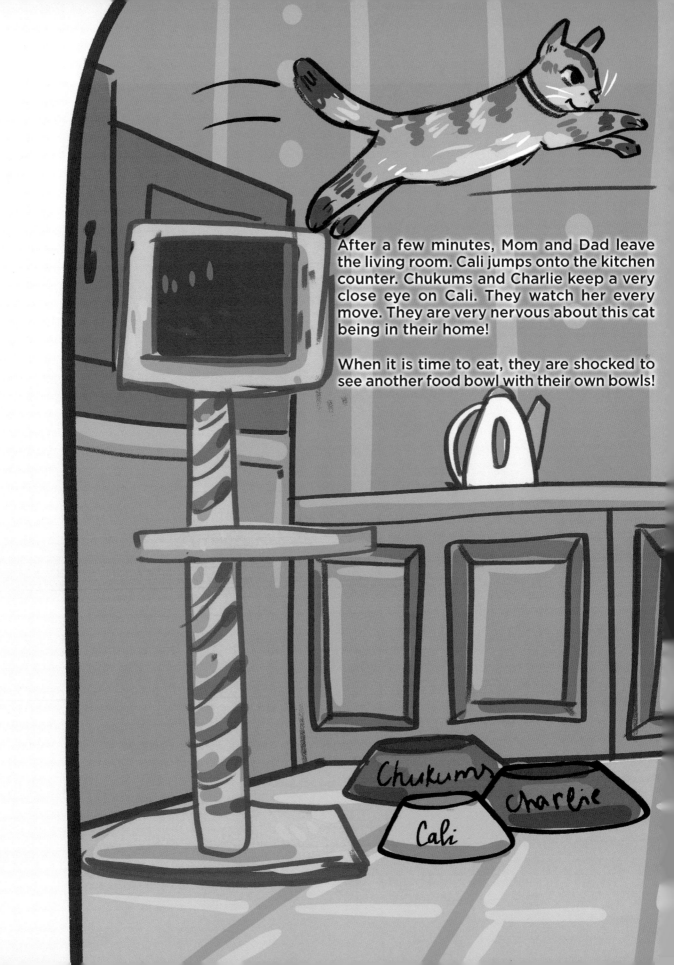

After a few minutes, Mom and Dad leave the living room. Cali jumps onto the kitchen counter. Chukums and Charlie keep a very close eye on Cali. They watch her every move. They are very nervous about this cat being in their home!

When it is time to eat, they are shocked to see another food bowl with their own bowls!

Chukums

Charlie

Cali

Later, when they return home after their walk, Cali is waiting for them at the front door. Despite her sisters' feelings, she still tries to play with them.

"Would you like to play a game of tag with me?" she asks, but Chukums and Charlie bark and try to bite her! Cali runs away.

The next day, Chukums and Charlie are playing in the backyard. They make sure to give a few growls to keep Cali away. Dad is busy inside the house and Mom is swimming in the pool. Some leaves begin moving in the tree.

On alert, Charlie says, "We better go check out that noise!" They run to the tree to see what is happening.

Suddenly, a raccoon barrels out of the tree, making all kinds of scary noises! Poor Chukums and Charlie are scared. This raccoon is not very friendly. Cali comes running; she is not afraid! She meows and hisses so ferociously that the raccoon is terrified and runs right back up the tree.

Cali has a distinctively wild look that no raccoon wants to tangle with!

From that moment on, something happens. Chukums and Charlie thank Cali. They tell her, "You are family because you protected us."

Cali purrs and rubs herself on Chukums and Charlie.

"All I wanted was to be loved and to be part of the family," she says. Chukums and Charlie understand. Even though Cali is a cat, she has feelings. She wants to be accepted. They realize that having another sister might even be fun!

Well, they are right! Cali is curious and playful. Cali taps Charlie on the nose to get her to play. It works! As Cali runs fast around the house, she leaps right over Chukums. In mid-air, she taps Chukums on the back to get her to play along, too. She even tries to get Chukums and Charlie to play by passing her ball to them, "Here, catch!"

Smiling and laughing, they tell Cali, "You are fun to play with!" They even discover that playing tag in the backyard is more fun when Cali plays, too. And when they get thirsty, they even stop to share a drink from the water fountain. After getting along with their new sister, Chukums and Charlie are eager to teach Cali a thing or two.

"We love to do tricks for treats, just watch!"

Mommy and Daddy say, "Sit pretty and show me your paw." When they hold up a paw, they are rewarded with a treat. Before long, Cali is holding up a paw, too!

They begin doing everything together! They even sleep next to each other. In fact, Cali sleeps in the doggie beds with her sisters. Chukums and Charlie really like to snuggle with her.

Not only do Chukums, Charlie, and Cali become friends and love one another, but more importantly, they realize that they are family! They all learn how important families are. As their mom and dad say, "It doesn't matter who is in your family. It matters that everyone in your family is united, loved, and that they protect one another."

Chukums, Charlie, and Cali couldn't agree more!

The End

Three hearts, two dogs, one cat = Fur-Ever Family

This book is a tribute to my beloved long-haired Chihuahuas named Chukums and Charlie. Chukums, Charlie and Cali truly shared an unbreakable bond. Cali loved, learned from, and looked up to her doggie sisters. We as a family, are so thankful and value the years we shared with Chukums and Charlie. They showed us unconditional love and were such a special part of our lives. We miss our beloved Chihuahuas, who we will *fur-ever* hold in our hearts.

Follow us! Instagram @chukumscharliecali